The Addiction

By Jaid Black

Chapter One

"Come on, Lynette, be a friend. I need this job!"

"Shel—"

"Don't say it! Do not say I'm fired! I'll try harder. I promise!"

"It's not a matter of trying harder, honey. I don't think there are enough pole dancing classes in the world to help you. I love you to death, but you are the worst stripper I've come across in over fifteen years in the business."

Shelli Rodgers watched Lynette wear a hole in the carpet as her friend and boss frenetically paced back and forth. A cigarette dangled from Lynette's Botox-injected lips as she strutted around in her well-manicured, and very black, office.

Shelli paused, momentarily distracted from the guillotine that loomed over her head. She supposed the black walls, plush ebony carpet, and dark-as-midnight ceiling were an accurate reflection of Lynette's current and usual abysmal mood, but how could anybody like this much black? It was depressing.

"Look," Shelli began, her violet eyes beseeching. She ran a hand through her dark-brown hair, which seemed light in comparison to the office. She moved toward Lynette. "I know everything you say is true, but I—*oomph!*"

She could hear Lynette's long-suffering sigh as Shelli picked herself up from the floor. She winced, realizing that faux pas wasn't about to win her boss over. Why did the chairs have to be the same color as everything else in this wretched room?! Damn it.

"You see!" Lynette's nostrils widened as she threw her hands up in dismay. "This is exactly what I'm talking about. You have no grace, zero coordination, and I've seen full-body vomiting that's more attractive."

"I'm not that bad," Shelli muttered, frowning.

"Yes!" Lynette shrieked, still pacing. "Yes you are!"

"Okay, maybe I am!" Shelli straightened to her full five feet ten inches, which would have been five feet four inches without benefit of the stripper stilettos she wore. Or tried to wear. She'd broken more than a few pairs. "But I still need this job. I really, really need it." How *did* Lynette keep that cigarette's long ash from breaking off and falling onto the carpet? Had it been Shelli, the fire department would have already been dispatched. "Another six months and I'll have my Ph.D. in Anthropology. You'll be rid of me forever, I promise!"

Six months. All Shelli needed was six lousy months and she'd never have to impose upon their friendship again. If there was another job she could work making the same money for the same scant hours per week, she would have moved on long ago. But there wasn't. Not even the world's worst stripper made bad tips. Unless the club patrons demanded their money back, of course. But that had only happened a few times.

Lynette tugged in a long, seemingly cathartic drag of the cigarette. The damn ash still dangled.

"Please," Shelli implored, her violet gaze desperate. "Just one more chance?"

Lynette sighed. She moved the cigarette from her lips to the first two fingers of her left hand. Shelli watched in amazement as the ash held firm.

"All right," Lynette ground out. "One more chance. But this is it, Shel." Her eyes narrowed. "I mean it."

Shelli smiled, relieved and elated. "You won't regret it!"

"I somehow doubt that."

She ignored the slight. "I'm sorry about tonight. I didn't mean to fall into Mr. Rivera."

"Falling into him wasn't the problem," Lynette said, exasperated. "Falling into him and knocking a burning-hot cup of coffee onto his lap was the problem!"

"It couldn't have been too hot," Shelli muttered, her cheeks going up in flames. "It also splattered onto his friend's lap and his friend didn't complain."

"That's because he couldn't feel it! For fuck's sake, Shel, he sits in that wheelchair because his legs are paralyzed. It isn't a fashion statement!"

"Maybe it should be," Shelli sniffed, feeling defensive. "The chair matched his suit quite nicely."

Lynette looked ready to strangle her. Perhaps it was time to shut up.

"Thanks again," Shelli enthused, smiling cheerfully. "I'll practice on the pole before work tomorrow." She made her way to the office door, this time without tripping. "See? I'm getting better already."

The cigarette was back in her boss's mouth. Lynette's eyes closed as her hands moved to her temples, rubbing them.

"Did something give you a headache? You should take some aspirin."

Lynette's eyes flew open. The ash broke and fell to the carpet.

"Right," Shelli squeaked. She swallowed heavily. "I'll see you tomorrow."

Chapter Two

He was tired.

His life, his business ventures, his houses, his cars, his women, his friends — all of it.

Friends, he breathed, his hands fisting and unballing at his knees. A better word would be users. Or vultures.

He only had one real friend in this world and that was Jack McKenna. It felt like ages since they'd hung out together and in truth, probably would be ages before they could again. At least they were tentatively scheduled to have a drink together tomorrow while John was on the mainland. *Scheduled!* What had life become when it's necessary to schedule a drink with your best buddy?

That was the shitty part about growing up and becoming adults. Too much work and no time to appreciate the fruits of your labor.

John Calder sat in the back of his limousine, his blue gaze absently staring out the window. Nothing gave him joy anymore. Nothing.

Once upon a time he had aspired to great wealth. He had long ago obtained it. Once upon a time he had set out to be so powerful a man that he could have any famous woman he desired. He'd had them all, a few times.

The problem with dreams, John decided, is that once you fulfilled them there was nothing left to inspire you, no reason to get out of bed in the morning, no new challenges waiting to be conquered. Every new day becomes as monotonous as the one before it, every superficial woman as boring as her predecessor.

His cell phone rang, snagging his attention from the San Francisco landscape whizzing by outside the vehicle. He glanced at the caller ID.

"Daisy Renee Halcomb," he muttered, tossing the cell phone onto the unoccupied space next to him. "Emmy-winning actress now setting her sights on Broadway. I've got news for you, Daisy, you're not talented enough for Broadway."

Nobody was there to listen to his ranting so it didn't matter how unapologetically truthful he was. "You're not only boring, but vain as well."

She could give a decent blowjob, though. Daisy Renee should have set her sights on low-budget porn or on working at John's *Hotel Atlantis* resort. At least then she stood a reasonable chance at not getting booed off stage.

The window separating chauffeur from passenger glided down. John arched an inquisitive dark-gold eyebrow at his driver of ten years. Manuel was a good guy and, John admitted, a good friend. Because of their age gap, their relationship was more like father-and-son than a friendship in the conventional sense, but the older man was good people and John could always rely on him.

"You sure you want to hit the clubs right away? You should eat," Manuel chastised.

John sighed. "No choice, Manny. We're short three girls."

Manuel returned his look with an arched brow of his own. The man understood him too well.

"I know there's still plenty of time, but what the hell else do I have to do? Never mind, don't answer that."

There was no encouraging reply to be stated, after all. John had nothing to do and they both knew it. Work was all John Calder had. Forty years old and he still had no wife and children to go home to, nobody special to grow old with.

You brought this on yourself. Your entire world is of your own making.

John ignored his thoughts and looked back out the window. At least he had his work. That was worth something.

Or it used to be, anyway.

* * * * *

His blue gaze flicked up to the neon-lit marquee. *Venus Rising*. Yep, this was the place Jack had told him about. The best strippers in California, he'd promised.

A small smile tugged at John's lips. His buddy Jack's idea of a great stripper was any woman who'd show him her tits. Still, it was worth checking out. God knows he'd been to almost every other club in the state at one time or another.

Manuel opened the front door to the establishment. The familiar scent of booze and smoke wafted into their faces like a cloud.

"You coming in, Manny?" John inquired, already knowing the answer.

Manuel shook his head. "I'll stay with the car."

John nodded. "Hopefully this will be quick. We can grab a beer afterward."

"Best offer I've had all night."

"I somehow doubt that, with pretty Angelina waiting for you at home," John replied, "but nice try."

Manuel's chuckle made him smile again. Two smiles in one night. It had to be a record.

Making his way past the club's entrance, John paid the requisite cover charge and continued deeper into *Venus Rising*.

11

The pulsating sound of techno-pop music blared loudly, the frenzied beat in tune with the strobe lights. An expensive fog machine worked overtime, giving the club a vampirish feel. It must have been the vibe the establishment's owner had been going for. All the topless barmaids sported gothic, cupless bustiers, leather G-strings and, he noticed as he squinted for a better look, fangs.

Vampires. He rolled his eyes. So overdone.

A well-dressed bouncer of John's acquaintance nodded at him, beckoning for him to come closer. He couldn't remember the guy's name, but recognized his face as that of a former employee. The man had left John's private island in good standing. If memory served, the bouncer's mother had become ill and he'd found it too difficult to commute back and forth from the mainland to the island on an ongoing basis.

Funny. He could recall all those details, but couldn't remember the man's name.

"Mr. Calder," the bouncer said, smiling. "It's me, Mike. You remember?"

Everything but your name. "Of course. How have you been? How is your mother?"

The bouncer seemed surprised that John would remember any details about his life. But then, most people assumed the controversial John Calder was an arrogant, unfeeling asshole concerned with nobody's welfare but his own.

He supposed they had good reason to assume it. Despite his numerous business holdings and vast wealth that sprang from a sophisticated stock portfolio, it was his notorious role as what amounted to a pimp that kept his name in the media.

Hotel Atlantis was situated on John's lush, private island off the coast of San Francisco, just far enough into international waters to make prostitution legal. The women in his employ could hardly be thought of as streetwalkers, though, for they made enviable sums of money that would make most CEOs blush. John kept them well-protected, provided them with the world's richest gentlemen clientele and looked after their well-being in an almost fatherly fashion. But no matter how nicely he dressed it up, he was still a pimp.

That title didn't used to bother him. Lately, it disturbed him a lot.

"My mom's doing real good," Mike said, smiling. "She has her bad days, but she's a fighter. The cancer's in remission."

"I'm very happy to hear that."

Mike inclined his head. "The VIP section is over here. Come on, I'll get you a private table."

"Thank you."

Again the bouncer seemed surprised. This time because of two simple words — *thank you*. Mike looked at John as though he was no longer certain who he was.

Did I come across that bad back then? Was I so caught up in making the next business deal that I forgot basic manners?

Probably, John conceded. Up until about six or seven months ago it had always been about the money.

Mike led him to a private viewing area toward the front of the club. He nodded his thanks at the bouncer before seating himself at the secluded table. If there was one good thing that had come of his infamous reputation, it was that John Calder always got the best seat in the house no matter where he was.

"Mike says you're a bourbon man." Lost in his thoughts, John almost didn't hear or notice the barmaid who stood over him. He glanced up, her bared tits at his eye level. "So here's a bourbon on the house, Mr. Calder. Compliments of the owner, Lynette Shofield."

John's assessing gaze raked over her bared breasts. Her nipples plumped up at his perusal. "Please thank Ms. Shofield for me," he murmured. He lifted the glass. "Cheers."

The barmaid wet her lips. "Cheers." She thrust her breasts closer to his face. "Holler if you need me," she said thickly.

John nodded then looked away. She wanted to fuck him. No surprise there. She had been told who he was, after all.

Chapter Three

High heels in hand, Shelli jogged toward *Venus Rising* as quickly as her tennis shoes could carry her. Time had gotten away from her back at San Francisco State. She'd been so embroiled in writing up her proposal for the dissertation committee that the passing hours had felt more like minutes.

Lynette would not be pleased. Ordinarily her boss didn't mind when she was running a little late on account of her university classes, but Shelli reasoned every mistake she made tonight would likely grate on Lynette's nerves after last evening's hot-coffee fiasco. Not to mention the fact that Shelli had promised to practice on the pole before the club even opened.

No. Lynette definitely would not be a happy camper.

I wish I didn't need this job. I wish Lindsay would get her head out of her ass and help Mom make ends meet until I graduate!

Shelli exhaled as she ran full throttle ahead. Maybe it wasn't fair to even semi-blame her sister for the mess Dad's death had left the whole family in, but now that he was gone, everyone needed to pitch in and help. Shelli hated working at *Venus Rising* as much as Lynette hated employing her, but she was doing what needed to be done. Not that Shelli wanted

Lindsay working alongside her, getting groped by drunk, ugly men, but hell, even a part-time job at McDonald's would have gone a long way toward helping the family out.

Lindsay had always been the self-involved sister, the one so tightly wrapped up in herself that it was a wonder she could breathe. But despite that flaw, she had never been one to turn her back on the family when they needed her, either. Her behavior since their father's death was unpredictable at best and shameful at worst.

"Hey, watch where you're going!"

"Careful, bitch!"

Shelli ignored the belligerent shouts of the people she'd accidentally barreled into and kept running. If they hadn't been so nasty, she would have taken the time to stop and apologize, but their attitudes made them unworthy of further tardiness from work. Lynette would be pissed enough.

Six more months, Shel. You can hang in there for six damn months. And when it's over, you will never look back.

* * * * *

Boring. The only word that came to mind to describe *Venus Rising* was boring.

John sighed, wondering not for the first time if he'd simply become too jaded. All of the girls were pretty enough, some might even say beautiful. Yet none of them had managed to snag his attention, let alone pique his curiosity.

"You're here to find hookers," he muttered to himself, picking up his bourbon to finish it, "not a fucking soul mate."

The music changed and a new trio of dancers appeared on stage, each of them working their own pole. Two fanged blondes and one fanged brunette. John rolled his eyes, quickly tiring of the vampire theme.

The blondes were typical strippers, their routines in sync and well-rehearsed. They looked good, danced beautifully, and still he felt nothing. Depressed, he decided it was time to quietly make his exit. Maybe a good night's sleep would put him in a better mood. Assuming he could fall asleep. Insomnia had been his constant companion for months now.

John stood to leave, then paused as a loud *boom* snagged his attention. He glanced up at the stage, immediately noticing that the stripper working the middle pole—the brunette—had taken a fall. Instinctively he took a step toward her to help, but stopped as she stood up and continued gyrating as though nothing had happened.

One eyebrow rose. Curious, John sat back down.

He watched the brunette dance—or try to dance, was more to the point—for the next fifteen minutes. She was a beautiful woman with dark hair and Elizabeth Taylor eyes. Her body was lush and provocative, curvy in all the right places. Big tits, round ass—gorgeous. But her dancing...

She didn't belong up there. That realization intrigued him all the more.

For the first five minutes John had wondered if all the falls and klutzy mistakes had been done on purpose, though he'd never heard of comedic stripping. It became rapidly apparent that, no, the horrific pole work was not an act and the brunette simply couldn't dance to save herself. When her fangs fell out and landed in a patron's expensive drink, well, that was the capper.

John's mouth curved into a smile. She definitely didn't belong up there.

He pulled out a crisp one hundred dollar bill and held it up so she'd see him and come closer. The blondes swarmed him like vultures, but he paid them no attention as he waited on the brunette to notice him. She never did. She was too busy biting her tongue in concentration as she danced—if one stretched the meaning of the word far enough—around the pole.

The two blondes prudently scurried over to different customers, aware that they wouldn't be getting that bill out of John's hand. His gaze was fixed on the clumsy brunette. When the object of his interest fell down and banged her knees for what had to be the fourth time, she managed to break one of her stilettos in the process. John grinned as he watched her take the shoes off and mutter something undecipherable under her breath. Barefoot, she continued to attack the pole, trying to climb up it for reasons unknown. It brought to mind an injured monkey attempting to get up a tree.

He chuckled. Comedic stripping had its values.

Wondering what she would do next, he was more than a little disappointed when the routine came to an abrupt end and the lights on stage faded to black. He decided to wait around for the next show, hoping she would be in it. If not, he'd find the owner and unsubtly ask for an introduction. He wasn't worried that minor formality would be denied— nobody ever told him no.

John inclined his head toward a waitress, indicating he wanted another bourbon. Shifting in his seat, it occurred to him that the brunette had kept him smiling, even laughing, for fifteen straight minutes.

She was the lousiest stripper he'd ever seen. She was awkward, accident-prone and danced like a rabid animal.

But she was also a miracle worker.

Chapter Four

Shelli was afraid she'd end up getting fired from the moment her fangs popped out. When the heel of her stiletto broke and she spent the rest of the routine dancing barefooted, well, she knew she was toast at that point. And she was right. Lynette handed her the proverbial walking papers within seconds of making it backstage. Shelli had realized there was no point in begging her ex-boss to let her keep the job. She sucked at stripping. Worse, an important client had been in the audience to witness all of tonight's mishaps. She might have cost Lynette some business deal or another.

John Calder. Shelli'd heard the name, of course, but had no idea which of the many men in the audience he had been. School kept her too busy to read tabloids or watch much television.

The male patrons all seemed to blend together in her mind anyway. They always had. The only man tonight who stood out from the others had been a really handsome blond guy seated toward the front. It wasn't his looks that had struck her, though. It was the quiet sadness in his eyes. She'd watched him from backstage before what had turned out to be her final show, but had no idea why she'd fixated on him in particular.

It had to be the eyes. They lent a certain vulnerability to an otherwise physically intimidating man.

Shelli frowned severely. She was probably being dramatically romantic. It wouldn't have been the first occasion. The last time she thought she'd seen vulnerability in a man's eyes it had turned out to be conjunctivitis.

Taking a deep breath, she pushed all contemplations of the brooding stranger out of her mind. Staring out the taxi's window, she turned her thoughts to finding a new part-time job. Try as she might, she couldn't think of any job but stripping that paid like a fulltime occupation while requiring half the hours.

There will be no more stripping!

Not that anyone in their right mind would hire her for it. Shelli rubbed her temples, feeling uncharacteristically dismal. Six months! That's all she needed. Her dream job awaited her once she earned her Ph.D.

The university was closing down after tomorrow's classes for a three-week holiday break. Thank goodness she had a mother to stay with because that meant the dorms were closing too, even the small facility that a few lucky graduate students got to keep residence in.

It also bought her time to find a new job. Somehow, Shelli decided, everything would work out, if for no other reason than it had to. In half a year she *would* be an anthropologist with a real career. She'd busted her ass for eight years and some change to make that dream a reality.

She wasn't good at stripping for people, but she was damn good at studying them.

* * * * *

He was becoming more than a little irritated.

John cursed under his breath as he listened to the dorm security guard tell Manuel that all the students had left campus for winter break, including the graduate students. He was beginning to wonder if his brunette — Shelli — would ever be found.

When she hadn't come out to perform another dance, John had immediately sought out the owner of *Venus Rising*. It had taken some doing, not to mention some cash, but he'd managed to finagle Shelli Rodgers' name and address out of the woman who had fired her.

"Are you crazy?" Lynette had sputtered out. *"You can't possibly want Shelli to work at Hotel Atlantis. She'd probably trip and puncture somebody's scrotum with her stilettos!"*

John half-snorted at the remembered warning. Lynette might have been right, but then, he had no interest in employing his brunette to fuck a man who wasn't him. He didn't even know what it was about her that drew his interest like a moth to a flame. She was pretty, yes, but he'd had pretty many times.

She made you smile. She forced you to enjoy being alive for fifteen straight minutes…

He wanted that feeling back. Even if it was only for another fifteen minutes.

"You okay, boss?"

John's head shot up. How could he be okay? He was irrationally obsessed with a woman he'd never so much as spoken to. If he ever found her, which was beginning to look like a very big if, she might turn out to be as boring and shallow as every other woman of his acquaintance.

He inclined his head toward Manuel. "I'm fine."

The driver frowned, obviously not believing him. "You might not be now, but you will be soon."

John's right eyebrow rose inquisitively.

"The security guard should be fired, but he told me exactly where to find Ms. Rodgers. Her mother lives about an hour's drive away and that's where she goes when the dorms close."

A dull pain flickered to life in John's chest. Any other man might have called it hope or pleasure. John was simply grateful to feel anything at all. "Excellent work," he murmured.

Manuel nodded. "Shall we go?"

"No. I'll go alone."

"You sure? I don't mind."

"You never mind, which I appreciate. But go home to Angelina. I'll take things from here."

Manuel's smile came slowly. "You got it that bad for the lady?"

"I don't even know the lady!" John snapped. He grunted, offended. "And yes."

Chapter Five

"I ain't eatin' this horse shit."

"Mama—"

"Don't 'Mama' me, Vanessa Ann Rodgers. I hate restaurant food, always have. I guess I could pick a booger out of my nose and eat that. Lord knows it'll taste better."

"Grandma!" Shelli half scolded and half laughed. She'd learned long ago there was no sense in getting embarrassed over her feisty grandmother's antics, but said grandmother was making the face of her daughter—Shelli's mom—heat up from all the unwanted attention their table was drawing. "Be nice! Mom's treating you to a dinner out so you don't have to cook."

"I like cookin', always have. I cooked for your granddad every night for forty-seven years before he up and died on me."

"I know, Mama," Vanessa said patiently, "but you can cook tomorrow night, can't you?"

"I'm with Grandma," Shelli's sister Lindsay announced. She stood up, eyeing the plate disdainfully. "This steak is garbage."

Shelli's nostrils flared. She wasn't in love with the food in this dive either, but there was no use in hurting their mom's feelings. She'd worked her ass off to pay for this outing. Lindsay worked her ass off for no one. "Beggars can't be choosers."

Lindsay rolled her eyes. "Whatever." She picked up her purse and hoisted it over one shoulder. "See you later, Miss Perfect."

"Where are you going?" their mother demanded.

"Out with friends."

"What time will you be home?"

"When I get there."

Furious, Shelli looked away from her sister before she said something they'd all regret. In the two days she'd been back home, all they seemed to do was fight. Sighing, she absently glanced around the diner. Luckily, the interest surrounding Grandma's rant had apparently waned. The other customers seemed wrapped up in their own conversations again.

A curious feeling stole over Shelli, a ripple of awareness that alerted her to the fact someone was watching her. She scanned the small diner again. Nothing.

"What's going on with Lindsay?" Shelli asked as she turned to watch her sister leave the diner. "Her behavior is terrible, Mom. Even for her."

Vanessa sighed. "I wish I knew. It's been this way since Daddy died."

"And getting worse," Shelli muttered.

"Give her time," Grandma cut in. "Everybody's got to deal with things in their own way and in their own time."

"I suppose you're right," Shelli said. "But I worry for her. She's not on drugs, is she?"

"No, no, nothing like that," Vanessa assured her.

"Positive?"

"Completely."

Shelli nodded. Her mom would know. She'd spent thirty-three years married to a drug addict, after all. Dad had tried to kick his addiction for years. In the end, the addiction had kicked him into an early grave.

Every time circumstances forced Shelli into remembering her dad's overdose, conflicting emotions were the inevitable result. Her brain, the logical part of her, recognized that her father had a horrible disease. But her heart, that damn organ mislabeled as being responsible for emotions, well, it had a mind of its own. Her heart believed that Dad should have loved his family more than getting high and feared that maybe he hadn't.

She sighed. Perhaps Lindsay's behavior wasn't surprising after all. She undoubtedly experienced the same contradictory emotions that, unbidden, still wreaked havoc on Shelli. Regardless, Lindsay was only two years younger than Shelli's twenty-nine. It was time to woman up and become a productive member of the family again.

Shelli blinked. That weird feeling was back. The sound of her mom and grandma bickering back and forth was drowned out by an acute awareness that someone was watching her. She scanned the diner another time.

Still nothing. Shelli frowned, wondering why that bizarre alertness persisted. Nobody was paying her any attention at all. Everyone was minding their own business and embroiled in their own conversations. She looked down to her plate.

"Horse shit," Grandma announced. She patted her overly bleached beehive into place. "Let's demand your money back, Vanessa Ann. I'll cook at home."

Shelli smiled at her grandmother's words as she glanced up. Her gaze clashed with a handsome blond man's. It was obvious he had overheard Grandma because he had an entertained look about him. She amusedly rolled her eyes at the stranger, giving him a *what-can-you-do-about-ornery-grandmas* look. He smiled back.

Shelli stilled. She squinted thoughtfully. There was something very familiar about that man, about those blue eyes...

Comprehension slowly dawned. Her eyes rounded.

Shelli's pulse soared as the golden-haired Adonis held her stare. He was that man from her last night working at the club. Oh no! What the hell was he doing here? She hysterically wondered if he'd approach their table and say something idiotic to her mother and grandmother, something that would alert them to the fact she'd been taking her clothes off for money.

The man rose from his seat.

Shit! Shit! Shit!

"Maybe we should go home and let Grandma cook," Shelli breathed out, returning her gaze to her family. "I'm suddenly not feeling very well."

"You see, Vanessa? This horse shit done poisoned my baby."

Vanessa frowned at her mother before turning to her daughter. "Sweetie, what's wrong? You look like you just saw a ghost."

31

"I think I'm just tired. My dissertation work has me drained."

"See there, Vanessa? Don't worry, Shel. If your mama insists we gotta stay here then Grandma will pick you a good booger to eat. It'll be healthier than this mess."

Shelli simultaneously groaned, gagged and laughed. The man was getting closer by the second. He had to stand in the vicinity of six and a half feet. Two more strides on those long legs and he'd be here. There was no escape.

"Mama, enough! Shelli, are you okay, honey? We can go home."

It was too late anyway. "No, no, I'll be fine. I know this meal cost you money you don't have."

"Never mind that. My budget can survive one meal."

"Yes, Shelli," a male voice broke in, drawing everyone's attention, "her budget will be fine because as it turns out, the meal is free."

"Free?" Grandma inquired.

"Yes," the man returned. "The diner is having a special today. Free food for all tables with cranky old ladies."

Grandma sniggered then picked up a French fry and popped it into her mouth. "Still tastes like horse shit, but it's free horse shit."

Shelli's attention, until then fully on the familiar stranger, was ripped in half. At that moment she realized why her grandmother always made a fuss when they went out to eat. Because she knew her daughter couldn't afford it and she wanted to spare her pride. The realization damn near made her cry.

"Sir," Vanessa began, "that's awfully nice of you, but I can't—"

"Please," the man softly interrupted. "I'd be honored to pay for the meal. Besides, you don't want your mother clearing out her nose for all the world to see, do you?" He winked. "Plus I'm a friend of your daughter's and I owed her one."

Shelli's world suddenly seemed very, very small and shrank further with every heartbeat. He owed her one? That had an ominous ring to it. What had she done to him?

Shit! Shit! Shit!

She searched her memories, trying to recall if she'd ever dumped hot coffee on his lap or accidentally whipped him in the eye during one of the bondage routines. Her sense of dread heightened. He wasn't the man whose scrotum she'd punctured with one of her stiletto heels, was he?

Oh God! Please don't be him! And if you are him, please tell me the surgeon was able to save your balls!

Stripping. What the hell had she been thinking?!

"Shelli! Why didn't you introduce us to your friend?" her mother chastised.

Shelli could barely form a coherent thought. Speaking was not an option.

"My name is John," the man offered, drawing the attention back to him. "John Calder."

Shelli's violet eyes widened. John Calder. The John Calder whom she had somehow managed to offend to the point of Lynette not getting to do business with him?

Holy shit. This could be worse than the scrotum incident.

* * * * *

"I just don't understand why you invited him to dinner," Shelli muttered to her mother. She continued peeling the potatoes as Grandma had instructed. "I was looking forward to a nice, quiet break at home with my family."

"It's one evening," Vanessa replied. "And he's your friend, isn't he?"

"Of course he is," Shelli said quickly. She wasn't about to contradict anything he'd told her family until she could get

34

him alone and find out why he was here and what he was up to. "I'm just tired and grumpy. Sorry, Mom."

Vanessa smiled, but said nothing.

An hour later the doorbell rang. Yesterday's feeling of impending doom once again settled over Shelli. Her pulse quickened as she heard her mother welcome John Calder into their home.

Shelli took a deep breath and slowly exhaled. There was no sense in reacting to him like this. If he was here for revenge, making her sweat would only delight him. Plus there was always the small, extremely remote possibility that he had no intention of ratting her out to her family. But if he wasn't here to sing like a bird then why was he here? Only revenge made sense.

Maybe he was as attracted to me as I was to him…

Yeah, right. She rolled her eyes at her own musings. Men only did romantic shit like following women home in the movies. Serial killers might do it too, she allowed. Either way, not good.

"Shelli, bring the damn mashed potatoes out here, girl!" Grandma yelled from the house's small dining room. "This boy needs to eat!"

Shelli snorted as she picked up the mashed potatoes with one hand and a pitcher of gravy with the other. Grandma always thought everybody needed to eat, most especially when she was the chef.

She took another deep breath, counted to ten and slowly exhaled. She just hoped this dinner sped by so she could find out why John Calder had followed her from San Francisco, and what it was he wanted from her. Steeling herself, she held her head high and exited the kitchen.

She was even more beautiful tonight than she'd been yesterday at the diner, which was saying a lot. Last night she'd worn makeup and a cute little dress that clung to all her sexy curves. Here at her house, she was makeup free and clothed in loose-fitting white exercise pants that hung just below her navel. Her white t-shirt, which sported a black logo he didn't recognize, should have left everything to the imagination, but her large breasts kept that from happening, leaving her midriff exposed. Her long, dark, wavy hair was haphazardly piled on top of her head, giving her a disheveled, recently fucked appearance.

John shifted in his chair. He hoped like hell he wasn't asked to stand up for whatever reason because there would be no hiding his erection.

"What's with the suit?" Shelli's grandmother asked, drawing his attention. "We're simple folk 'round here. No need for all that."

"Mom," Vanessa said under her breath, though John could hear her. "Please be on your best behavior in front of Shel's friend."

"Well hells bells, Vanessa Ann," the feisty matriarch countered in her usual loud voice. "What did I say wrong now?"

"Good grief, Grandma," Lindsay said, frowning.

Vanessa emitted a long-suffering sigh.

* * * * *

John glanced at Shelli, who stared back at him like a deer caught in headlights. He winked at her before turning his attention to her grandmother. "I had hoped to impress you with one of my best suits, Mrs. Rodgers. I suppose I'll have to think of another way to do that."

With the loud red lipstick, hopelessly out-of-style hairdo and horned glasses that bespoke of decades gone by, the older lady's grin could make anybody chuckle. Even a man who'd been dead inside for so long.

"I ain't Mrs. Rodgers, that old bitch died back before my Vanessa married her son. I'm Mrs. Vincent. But you can call me Arlene."

The eyebrows of all females at the dinner table rose in disbelief. Apparently their matriarch didn't permit most people to call her by her first name. A sense of pride and accomplishment swelled in John's chest. Ironic as it was, winning Arlene over made him feel better than closing any business deal ever had. He just hoped her granddaughter would prove to be as amenable.

"Thank you, Arlene. And thank you for this food. It's incredible."

Her smile widened. John smiled back. He hadn't lied or even stretched the truth, though. He'd eaten at damn near every five-star restaurant on the planet and none of them could hold a candle to this home-cooked meal. Creamy mashed potatoes smothered in gravy, country-fried steak, green beans and corn fritters...it was heaven.

"So how do you know my daughter?" Vanessa chimed in. A dead ringer for Shelli, she was a beautiful lady who'd aged quite well. Her smile was as soft and unassuming as she appeared to be.

From his peripheral vision, John could see Shelli shifting in her chair. He had wondered why she hadn't gainsaid him back in the diner and now he understood. Her family didn't know that she had been supporting herself by stripping. The calculating businessman in him couldn't help but file that information away for later use, should the need to use it arise.

"We met at San Francisco State," John answered without missing a beat. "A good friend of mine owns the construction company that redesigned the Anthropology department's building."

Shelli cleared her throat. John didn't look away from her mother and grandmother, but could sense her apprehension. Clearly he had unnerved her. She now realized there was little about her he didn't know.

Good.

Vanessa nodded, satisfied with his answer, and the meal continued. The next hour seemed to fly by for John as they all traded stories, laughed and ate. The close-knit togetherness of this family was intriguing and fulfilling, even if it was as foreign to him as happiness. Shelli managed to let down her guard a time or two, laughing at some of Arlene's many stories and even a couple of his. Her dimples popped out when she laughed, making her impossibly more attractive.

Shelli wasn't the only one letting her guard down. John found himself not only giving truthful answers to the many questions asked of him, but expounding upon them and divulging memories of his own. He was careful to avoid certain topics, though. Specifically, his role as a glorified pimp.

All eyes were riveted on him as he told them amusing tales about everything from his last trip to the Congo to the time he was gored by a bull in Pamplona. The latter story was of particular interest to everyone, especially to the feisty old lady whose cackles grew on him more and more with each passing second.

"Right in the ass?" Arlene asked.

"Right in the ass," John confirmed.

She snickered and started to ask another question, but was interrupted by Shelli. He turned to look at her, knowing she would want to speak to him privately. He was surprised she had waited this long to make an excuse to get him alone. Her family didn't seem aware of her nervousness, but then neither did they realize she had a reason to be.

"Grandma, your pecan pie is probably done by now," Shelli said with what seemed a forced cheerfulness. "Would you excuse John and me for a moment before dessert?"

"Go on," Vanessa answered for her, smiling. "I'll get the coffee going while Grandma sees to the pie."

John stood up when Shelli did. "I can hardly wait for dessert," he told the table. "I've never tasted homemade pecan pie before."

Arlene clucked her tongue as though he'd admitted a cardinal sin. Thank God she was clueless about the pimp part. "Go on and take a walk with my Shel. We'll fix your problem when y'all get back."

John couldn't help but be amused. From the way Arlene spoke, one would think he had a venereal disease or multiple heads rather than a lack of experience eating homemade pecan pie.

"We'll be right back," Shelli announced before turning to walk toward the front door. "We won't be long."

Chapter Six

Shelli didn't know what to think or how to feel. John Calder had been the perfect guest all through dinner. He hadn't said anything about *Venus Rising*, or even alluded to it. In fact, he'd been so pleasant and entertaining she'd almost found herself believing they were the friends he'd claimed them to be.

Except for the looks. She'd caught him staring at her more than once, his blue eyes raking over her face and breasts. She'd never felt so naked and aware of herself as she had in those moments. Not even up on a stage, where she'd worn nothing but a G-string and stiletto heels.

When they finally reached his car in the long gravel driveway, Shelli stopped and turned to look at John. He was so tall. And those muscles...not even an expensive Italian suit could hide them.

She took a deep breath and found the courage to meet his gaze. "What do you want from me?" she bluntly asked. There was no point in beating around the bush. "Why did you follow me here?"

His gaze bore into hers. He didn't answer for the longest time, so long in fact that she started to wonder if he ever would.

"I don't know," he murmured.

Shelli stilled. She wasn't certain how to respond. "You…you don't know?"

He shook his head, the movement almost imperceptible.

"Is it about Lynette? Are you angry that your business deal didn't go through? I'm sorry if I was the cause of that, but I assure you it wasn't—"

"Business deal?" John interrupted. He looked confused. "I don't know what you're talking about."

Their conversation grew stranger by the moment. "Lynette said something about a John Calder and my, uh, dancing, making her lose his business."

He snorted at that. His gaze, once distant, looked amused. "You're the worst stripper I've ever seen."

Shelli frowned. "I know!" she snapped. "But thank you for pointing that fact out."

"You made me laugh. I'd never seen a show quite so inept as yours."

Her cheeks reddened. She knew she was a lousy stripper, but hearing such a handsome man tell her he'd laughed at her performance still managed to sting her pride. Embarrassed and ashamed, she turned to walk away. A large, strong hand on her shoulder stopped her in her tracks.

"I didn't mean that in a bad way," John said quickly. "I can see how you'd take it like that, though."

Shelli's nostrils flared. She turned around and faced him once again. "You mean there's a *good* way to take that statement?"

That quiet sadness returned to his eyes, the same melancholia that had managed to attract and hold her attention as she'd watched him from backstage. This was the most bizarre conversation she's ever had. Logic dictated that the man was strange and she should run, yet her feet stayed firmly planted on the gravel driveway.

"I hadn't laughed in a long time," John said quietly. "It felt...well, it felt nice."

Silence.

Shelli's empathetic gaze raked over his face. "I'm sorry," she whispered.

He sighed and looked up to the stars. "I shouldn't have come here. I don't know why I did."

"It's okay," she assured him. She quietly cleared her throat. "I'm glad I managed to make you laugh." Her smile was self-depreciating. "Even if it was for all the wrong reasons."

John agitatedly ran a hand over his jawline before meeting her gaze. "I have to go. I've imposed long enough and I need to get some sleep tonight before driving back to the city tomorrow."

Shelli would have insisted he stay for dessert, but his earlier show of vulnerability had obviously embarrassed him. "Are you sure?"

His smile was beautiful yet painfully sad. "I'm sure," he murmured. Holding her gaze, he reached for her left hand and drew it up to his lips. The chaste kiss was headier than it had the right to be. "Thank you," he said softly. "For everything."

And then he was gone. Shelli watched him get into his Jaguar and drive away. Her gaze followed his car long after it had disappeared into the country night.

* * * * *

John turned off the shower. He slowly worked the cheap motel towel down the length of him, his every movement feeling heavy and surreal. Stepping into a pair of cotton pajama pants, he made his way to the motel room's small bed and fell down onto it. Staring at the ceiling, he asked himself for the hundredth time why he had driven away from the only woman in the world who had been able to make him feel alive in God knows how long.

Because she's too good for me. Because she doesn't belong in my world any more than I want to stay in it. Because watching that beautiful, dimpled face become as hard and jaded as my own would be a disservice to the entire planet.

John sighed. He'd made a lot of mistakes in his life, and becoming a pimp was the worst of them. He wasn't the type to bring a woman down to his level. Especially not the woman responsible for waking up something inside him, something that made him smile, laugh and want to live.

Something that felt a lot like hope.

Shelli tossed and turned in her bed, trying to get comfortable. No matter what position she rolled into or how many damn sheep she tried to count, sleep continued to elude her. Falling onto her back, she gave up the fight and let herself think about him.

John Calder. That strange, handsome, fascinating man.

No man had ever made her feel heartbroken for him just by looking into his sad eyes. No man had ever made her stomach knot and race with butterflies from a mere kiss on the hand. She smiled. No man had ever been so gentlemanly as to kiss her hand before.

"I hadn't laughed in a long time. It felt...well it felt nice."

His words played over and over again in her mind like a beautiful, broken record. To think that her clumsy pole dancing, of all things, was the impetus to his laughter, to following her back home for reasons even he didn't understand...

He might be toying with you, Shel. A man as powerful as him would know all the right moves in any game he chooses to play.

She bit her lip. Deep inside, she didn't believe that. Human behavior was her specialty and all her senses screamed that this man, this familiar stranger, was as broken and empty as his eyes promised he was. She could smell desperation from ten paces. Lord knows her father had reeked of it.

"I couldn't save Dad," Shelli whispered to the walls. "I sure as hell can't save John Calder."

Maybe he didn't need saving. Perhaps all John needed was a friend, someone to be there for him while he found the energy to surmount whatever mental hurdle had sent him chasing after a woman he didn't even know.

John had said he would be driving back to the city in the morning, which meant he was still here tonight. There was only a single motel anywhere in the area so she knew exactly where he had to be staying. Once he was gone, she might never get the chance to see him again. San Francisco was a huge metropolis, nothing at all like her Podunk hometown.

Shelli ran her fingers through her hair. What she was contemplating doing was sheer lunacy. He was a stranger whom she'd known for all of two days and she had spent a grand total of two hours with him.

"Thank you. For everything."

She was insane. He was insane. The entire situation was insane...

Shelli bolted upright and scurried out of bed to get dressed. Her mind was made up. Fumbling for the keys to her car, she quietly left the house so as not to wake anyone.

"I'm an idiot," she muttered to herself as she slid the key into the ignition. "John Calder, you better not be a serial killer."

At least she was certain he didn't have conjunctivitis. There was nothing pink about those haunting blue eyes.

Chapter Seven

There was nothing on television and John couldn't sleep. The insomnia refused to give him some peace, even when all his mental defenses were down. He hated being awake like this at night. It gave him too much time to think, too much time to ponder ideas that were selfish to even consider.

It would be so easy to end this. One well-placed bullet and no more pain. Who would I be hurting but myself?

Jack and his sister Sheri was who. Maybe even Manuel.

John sighed. He picked up the remote and switched off the television set. He was starting to feel like a vampire in a really dark movie. Too dead to feel alive, but unwilling to meet the dawn.

A knock on the motel room door startled him from his thoughts. Nobody knew where he was, so John couldn't imagine who it could be. He stood up and made his way to the door. If he was lucky it would be an armed robber who ended it all for him. The pain would be gone and he'd have had no hand in causing it.

"Yeah," he said, his voice monotone as he opened the door. "What do you—"

John stilled, completely caught off guard. But then, she was good at doing that to him. "Shelli?"

Shelli's heart pounded in her chest as she stared up at the very tall, half-naked man standing before her. It took a millisecond to ascertain that she had been correct about his musculature. Sweet lord above, he was beautiful. John Calder looked like he'd been chiseled from stone by Michelangelo himself.

He had the richly tanned skin of a man who spent a lot of time in the water. His chest was smooth, his nipples the sexiest she'd ever seen on a male. Her gaze lowered to where a line of dark-gold hair began just below his navel and trailed down into his pajama pants. His erection was long and thick, protruding against the fabric.

Her breath hitched. Her gaze flew up to meet his.

Neither of them spoke. Neither of them moved. Time seemed to stand still. His eyes were tinged with sadness, yet she could sense an even stronger emotion inside them fighting to win.

Her heart wrenched. He made her feel like he was a dying man and she was the only person on earth who could save him.

Shelli closed the door behind her, her gaze still locked with John's. Without a word, she began to undress. She lifted her shirt up and over her head, allowing her breasts to spring free. His eyes grew heavy-lidded, his breathing ragged, as he memorized her breasts with his gaze. Shelli tossed the forgotten garment to the floor as a knot of desire coiled in her belly and tightened her nipples.

She pushed down her exercise pants and G-string simultaneously, bending over slightly to discard them. Shelli kicked off her sandals then stood fully upright, her stare once again locking with his. John's gaze rose to her hair before lowering back down to meet her wide eyes. Understanding what he wanted, she raised her hands to the clip holding her loose bun in place and let it fall to the ground. Her long, dark hair pooled around her, cascading in wavy ringlets.

Her breathing grew heavier, causing her breasts to rise and fall. His eyes, once dead, seared with life. Shelli needed him to touch her like she needed air to breathe. She'd never desired any man like she did John.

She hoped she hadn't misread the situation and that he wanted her just as badly. The thought weakened her, leaving her to feel rawer and more exposed than she had ever felt before.

John stared down at Shelli, her stature so tiny compared to his. He was accustomed to tall models and actresses, but found himself preferring this height differential. Shelli might have been short, but there was nothing weak or vulnerable about her. Those attributes lay within him, he knew.

It scared John how much he needed this woman, a person who was all but a stranger to him. The feeling frightened him so powerfully that he found himself contemplating whether or not he should touch her. It would take only a single caress, he realized, and then he would be touching her all night long.

And then what about tomorrow? Touch her again? Bring this wonderful, generous woman down to his level? Make her life as wretched as his own had become?

John took a deep breath, hoping to regain control over the situation. But when he looked down and saw the fear of rejection dimming round, violet eyes that had always shone bright, it was his undoing. There was nothing inadequate about her, only about himself.

"John?" Shelli whispered. Her voice quivered almost imperceptibly.

She wanted him as much as he needed her. There was no fight left in him.

John reached out for her and Shelli flew into his arms. He picked her up and kissed her with all the hunger inside him, groaning when she wrapped her legs around his waist. He carried her to the bed as their tongues clashed and dueled, his mouth ravenously covering hers.

Falling with her onto the bed, John settled between her thighs as their kiss deepened and intensified. Shelli moaned and reached for his pajama bottoms, her hands working them down as far as they could manage before settling on his ass and squeezing. John groaned into her mouth, then broke their kiss long enough to get completely naked. He threw aside the unwanted clothing and settled back between her legs.

"John," Shelli panted, her face flushed, "John— I— Please."

She sounded as aroused and confused as he was. Like she wanted everything and more, but wasn't certain what *more* entailed.

His breathing heavy, John palmed Shelli's large breasts. The sound of her gasp made his balls tighten and his cock grow impossibly harder. Lowering his head, he pushed her tits together, giving his mouth access to both. She whimpered as his tongue curled around one of her stiff nipples and drew it into his mouth, then moaned as he began to suck it.

"Oh my God," Shelli breathed out, her voice coming in gasps, "Oh John — *Oh my God.*"

He growled around her nipple, having never felt so possessive of a woman in his life. He took his time, sucking on it from root to tip, her sounds of pleasure heightening his arousal. John released her nipple with a popping sound and covered the other one with his mouth. He sucked it hard, and harder still, her every moan forcing him closer to the edge.

He didn't want to come on her. He wanted to come *in* her.

His breathing heavy, John tore his mouth away from her nipple, a second heady popping sound underlining that fact. "You're so fucking sexy," he said thickly, grabbing his cock by the base. He settled himself between her legs as he guided his shaft to her wet opening. "I want you so damn bad, Shelli."

John stared into her wide eyes, waiting for her to say she wanted him just as much. Shelli didn't speak, but reared her hips at him instead, telling him without words everything he needed to know. He couldn't wait another second to be inside her. His jaw tight, John groaned as he surged deep inside her tight pussy.

Shelli's loud and immediate scream of pain startled him, forcing him to still within her. "Shel?" he murmured, his gaze once again locking with hers.

"I'm okay," she whispered, smiling up at him. "Just give me a second to adjust or something."

"But what's the mat —"

He blinked. His eyes rounded as comprehension slowly dawned.

Shelli blushed and looked away. John grabbed her chin and gently forced it back so she would see him.

"Yes," she said, her voice tinted with embarrassment, "I'm a virgin. Or I mean I *was* a virgin."

A virgin. A stripping virgin. Holy shit.

He wanted to say that she shouldn't feel ashamed, then show her he meant it by making slow, sweet love to her. He wanted to do and say a lot of things, but the primitive, territorial part of his brain could focus on one thing and one thing only...

No man had ever fucked her.

John began to move within her, trying to be gentle while realizing he was being anything but. Shelli accepted him anyway, her hands massaging his ass while he rutted inside her like an animal. "My pussy," John gritted out, his thrusts going deeper. "All mine."

"*John.*"

He rode her harder than he should have, her tight, sticky cunt sucking his cock back in on every outstroke. He'd fucked hundreds of women before, but none of them had made him feel as alive and important as he felt in this moment. None of them had made him feel anything at all.

He fucked Shelli harder, glutting himself on her cunt. The sound of wet flesh slapping against wet flesh filled the tiny motel room, heightening his arousal. His jaw tightened as he fucked her deeper and faster, over and over, again and again and again.

"I'm coming," John rasped out, his voice possessive and gravelly. He held onto Shelli tightly, his cock branding her pussy as his with each stroke. *"Here I come, baby."*

She bit his neck and squeezed his ass, sending him over the edge. John growled out his orgasm, his hips rapidly pistoning back and forth as his entire body shuddered and convulsed on top of hers. "Shelli — Jesus — *Shelli.*"

Shelli held him as he rode out the waves of pleasure, pulling him closer as he spurted his hot cum inside her. She whispered words he couldn't make sense of, but which comforted him nonetheless. Her arms wrapped tightly around him as he collapsed on top of her. They stayed that way for a long moment, neither of them speaking.

Finally, John slowly rolled off her, their embrace never breaking as he pulled Shelli to his chest. He needed to make love to her right, show her that he could do much better than rutting in her sweet pussy like an animal. Maybe then she'd never want to leave him.

It was his last coherent thought before succumbing to sleep.

* * * * *

Shelli awoke to the feel of her clit being gently lapped at. Her eyes flew open on a gasp. "John," she murmured, threading her fingers through his hair. "That feels so good."

Apparently *good* wasn't enough praise. His tongue curled around her sensitive clit and drew it into the heat of his mouth. She moaned, her hips instinctively rearing up. John pressed his face in closer, harder, and sucked on the aroused piece of flesh. Shelli groaned, the coiling knot of desire in her belly unlike anything she'd ever felt before. She'd experienced pleasure from masturbating, but no amount of self-stimulation could have prepared her for this moment.

John moaned around her clit, his lips and tongue working her into a frenetic state. She wrapped her legs around his neck, wanting his face pressed as tightly against her pussy as humanly possible. Her nipples stiffened as she hazily watched him suck on her.

"*Mmmm,*" John purred, sucking her clit in a steady rhythm, "*mmmmm.*"

The coil sprang loose. Shelli burst on a loud groan.

"*Oh my God!*" Shelli cried out. Her hips thrashed and her nipples jutted up impossibly farther. "*John!*"

He licked her, lapped at her, drank of her. Blood rushed to her face, heating it, then to her nipples and clit, making them beyond sensitive.

And still he didn't stop. He sucked on her aroused flesh again, forcing her body to a new, unchartered height where pain and pleasure mingled to become one. The next orgasm assaulted Shelli so hard she could barely remember her own name.

"*Oh John! Oh. My. Gohhhhhhd!*"

Shelli screamed out her orgasm, her entire body convulsing. She came violently, with a ferociousness she'd not known was possible. John praised her in moans as he lapped up her juices, his breathing growing heavy and his hands rubbing her thighs.

"I need you," she gasped, pulling at him, wanting him inside her. "Please."

John kissed his way up her body, from her navel to her lips, leaving nothing to neglect. He hovered over Shelli for a suspended moment, those haunting blue eyes piercing her soul. "Not like I need you," he murmured. Her eyes widened. He thrust inside her.

Shelli moaned, accepting him. She prepared herself for the same hard ride he'd given her their first time together, but John surprised her again. He plunged in and out of her slowly and steadily, letting her body adjust and learn. His cock was steel-hard, but his movements were controlled and gentle.

Shelli smiled into John's gaze as he made love to her.

* * * * *

They spent three more glorious days and nights together, never apart, both of them laughing, happy and complete. When they weren't joking around or making love, they had serious conversations about their lives, both of them being honest with the other about everything from their worst fears, to their jobs and schooling, even touching on sensitive subjects like religion and politics.

Yet despite their definite bond, regardless of the fact that his beautiful, haunted gaze had grown warm and alive, Shelli also knew John was guarding a part of himself. Whenever the moment grew too serious or too poignant, his blue eyes would lock up, as if searching for that dead space that was at once lonely and familiar to him.

She loved him. It was crazy—some would say impossible—to truly love someone after only a few short days, but Shelli was certain of her feelings. Female intuition whispered to her not to say the words, not to put her heart out there to get ripped to pieces, but in the end she decided that if he left her, that damn organ would get smashed to bits whether she'd been honest or not.

"I love you, John," Shelli said softly, accepting him inside her again. He stilled for a moment, but said nothing. "It's okay," she promised, stroking his back. "Just know that I do."

"Shelli...I—"

"Shhh." Her smile was genuine, making her dimples pop out. "I love you."

John groaned as he buried himself in her pussy. He made love to her as if his life depended on it, as if he was a dying man performing his final act on earth. On the fourth morning, Shelli knew why.

She awoke to an empty room, just as she'd feared she would one morning soon. The motel room was clean and everything that belonged to him was gone, as if she'd dreamt John's very presence there. Steeling herself against a wave of unwanted emotion and fighting back tears that threatened to spill, her gaze floated to the room's sole table, and to the note lying on it. She stood up and walked over to it, her heart heavy.

Dear Shelli,

I want to thank you for the best four days of my life. I realize this note is a cowardly way to end things, but I couldn't have held strong if we'd talked instead. Please trust me that this decision is for the best because you deserve a much better man than I'll ever be. I love you too, sweetheart, and I always will. That's why I have to let you go.

Forever, John

Shelli read the note at least a dozen times before lowering her gaze and clutching the piece of paper to her heart. Unable to stave off the inevitable a moment longer, she cried softly as hot tears streamed down her cheeks.

Chapter Eight
One Year Later

John Calder sat in the back of his limousine, his blue gaze watching the familiar scenery whiz by. It had been almost a year to the day since he'd last seen or spoken to Shelli, but in his mind it might as well have been yesterday. Not a day had gone by over the past twelve months that he hadn't thought about her, hadn't missed her. It had taken him far too long to get his shit together and evolve into a man worthy of her, but the former had come to pass even if the latter had not.

I know you must hate me, Shel. I just hope you can figure out a way to forgive me.

He glanced at his watch. Twenty more minutes and he'd reach her family's home.

Taking a deep breath and exhaling slowly, John wondered if Shelli even knew he was on his way. He'd spoken to her grandmother, Arlene, not to her.

Feeling increasingly nervous, John passed the remainder of the ride rehearsing every possible argument Shelli might throw his way to try to get him to go back from where he'd come. He couldn't do that, though—not again. He might have to spend the next ten years of his life getting her to understand that fact, but he was ready and willing to do whatever it took to get her back.

I need you, Shelli. I don't deserve you, but I need you…

John had gone through a lot to prepare himself for this moment in time. He'd wrestled with every mental demon a man can have and knew he was a better person for it. *Hotel Atlantis*, once the world's most expensive brothel, was now a relic of the past. He'd had the compound demolished and had taken great pleasure in watching as it smoldered down to cinders, smoke and ash. His best buddy Jack, the contractor he'd hired to do the deed, had been there beside him as he'd watched it go down. Jack understood the symbolism behind the act without either of them having to speak it aloud.

No more pimping. No more wondering how many marriages he'd ruined with that place. No more worrying that one of his former employees might have gotten emotionally scarred during her time as a prostitute.

No more overlooking every principle he'd once held dear in the name of a dollar.

Finally, John was at peace. The only part of the puzzle missing now was Shelli. He could only pray that somehow, some way, someday, she would forgive him.

* * * * *

"Girl, what did I say? I done told you not to contact the man! He needs to realize things on his own."

"She didn't, Grandma!" Lindsay sputtered in way of defense. "If you had listened while she spoke instead of thinking up your rebuttal, you'd know that."

"Oh horse pucky."

Shelli grinned at her sister from across the dinner table. Lindsay had done a lot of growing up in the past year and Shelli couldn't have been prouder. It was as if something inside Lindsay had finally snapped and awakened.

"It's true," Shelli's mom confirmed. "John has been contacting Shelli's boss, not Shelli."

"Dr. Torrence?" Grandma asked.

"Yes," Vanessa answered. "As it turns out, John's best friend Jack is married to Kris Torrence."

"*Jack*? Well I'll be damned."

"Yep," Shelli confirmed. "They're still newlyweds, actually. They got married about three months after I earned my Ph.D., right after I had Johnny."

Johnny. Shelli smiled from the mere thought of her son. Her unexpected pregnancy had shocked the entire family but it had also brought them closer together. She suspected that a huge part of Lindsay's transformation had come as a result of Shelli's beloved baby boy. Lindsay was turning out to be the world's greatest aunt and Johnny the planet's most spoiled nephew. Shelli wouldn't have had it any other way.

"So she's been married to Jack almost three months?" Grandma asked.

"Roughly," Shelli confirmed.

"I remember the stories you used to tell about the fights them two would have." Grandma shook her head. "How the hell did they go from that to saying their 'I-Dos'?"

Shelli shrugged, not in the mood to go into detail. Needless to say, the news of their marriage had thrown her for a loop too. But that was a different story altogether.

At any rate, her boss kept insisting that Shelli tell her who Johnny's father was. *"We are more than employer and employee,"* Krissy had harped, *"we're also friends."* Shelli had known that to be true so had confided in her as soon as she felt ready to tell the full story to someone outside her immediate family.

Shelli hadn't gotten quite the *"oh-my-God-I've-read-about-that-asshole-in-the-papers"* reaction that she'd expected. Instead, Krissy had been concerned for her *and* for John—she felt he should know about the baby he'd fathered. When Shelli admitted she didn't know how to contact him, so had named her son for him instead, Krissy had become giddy, bubbly and excited.

She knew John, as it turned out. She knew him quite well.

Stranger still was the doctor's insistence that things would work out, and John would see the error of his ways and come crawling back. The latter part had failed to happen, but at least John now knew of his son and wanted to see him. He had phoned this morning and asked Grandma if he could come out to the family house to talk to Shelli, so it seemed obvious Krissy had spilled the paternal beans. Grandma had told John, "it's about damn time," which was her surly way of saying yes.

A selfish part of Shelli wished that Krissy had been right and John was coming back into her life because he missed and needed her. But the biggest piece of her, the part called Mommy, was just glad her son had a father who wanted him. At least she hoped that was the case...

Shelli worried her lip. The troublesome thought that John might be coming to the house only to tell her he wanted nothing to do with their son permeated her consciousness for the first time. Her nostrils flared as feelings of anger and maternal protectiveness swept over her. Johnny was the center of her universe. If his father didn't feel the same way then he wasn't good enough to be in their lives anyway.

The doorbell rang, causing Shelli's heart rate to skyrocket. All eyes flew to her. She took a deep breath and slowly exhaled.

"Go on, girl," Grandma said, nodding her head. "He's either a man who done learnt a good lesson or a fool who needs to be sent away. Go see which it is. And be back here in time for my pecan pie."

Shelli pasted on a serene face and stood up. "You only make them at Christmastime, so I wouldn't miss a bite for the world."

Her hands felt clammy. She rubbed them together then smoothed out her jeans. Taking one last deep breath, Shelli made her way to the front door and opened it, but saw no one standing there. Frowning, she slipped outside, closing the door behind her.

Sensing someone's gaze boring into her, Shelli slowly turned her head. John stood next to the nativity scene in the front yard. He was dressed to the nines, as always, in what had to be an endless supply of designer suits. She should have felt frumpy in comparison wearing only jeans and a sweatshirt, but she didn't.

Somewhere between closing the door and making eye contact with him, her heartbeat had picked up again. Perhaps it was the smoldering way John was looking at her, studying her. Perhaps it was simply because she was in his presence again at long last. She bowed her head, feeling nervous as he approached.

"I love you, Shelli."

Her head shot up and her eyes widened. She hadn't expected that.

Their gazes clashed and held. She stared into his eyes, those beautiful, soulless eyes that always flickered with life in her presence. Her heart wrenched at his words, but she didn't know how she should feel or if he could be believed.

"I don't expect you to forgive me any time soon," John continued, his voice sounding raw with emotion, "but I can't let you go again. I don't care who you're dating or even if you're married. I can't live without you."

The look on his face was determined, his jaw set. She opened her mouth to speak, but nothing came out.

"God, I've missed you," he said hoarsely. "You are even more beautiful than I remembered in my fantasies, which is saying a lot."

"John," Shelli began, "please—"

"No!" he barked. "I'm begging you to tell me it's not too late! I'll never walk away again, Shel. *Never.*"

"John," Shelli said with quiet conviction, "I would never keep you from seeing him. You don't have to pretend to have feelings you don't in order to be in his life."

John blinked. "*His* life?" A possessive glare stole over his features. "Who," he asked icily, "is *he*?"

The wailing sound of a hungry three-month-old punctured the ensuing silence. John watched, his stoic expression unreadable, as Shelli's mom opened the door and handed their son to her. "I think he's ready for dinner," Vanessa whispered. She smiled at John before slipping back inside.

John didn't speak for a long moment. His gaze flicked back and forth between mother and son. Shelli grinned down at Johnny, his dark-gold hair standing straight up as though he'd been playing with a light socket. Once he was smiling, she looked back up at his father.

"You had a baby," John murmured, his eyes unblinking.

Shelli's nose wrinkled. He wasn't making any sense. "Well yeah."

They stood there in silence for a long minute. Finally John said, his voice filled with conviction, "I don't care. I'll raise him as my own."

What the hell are you talking about? "Raise him as your own?" Shelli repeated. *Have you gone insane?!* "I would hope so," she smiled, "since he *is* your own."

All color seemed to drain from John's face. Shelli's smile faltered and her eyes widened as the truth hit them both at the same time. John Calder was a father and hadn't even known as much until this very moment. She took a cue from him, fairly certain her own color was draining at a rapid rate.

"Kris didn't tell you?"

"No," he rasped.

"Oh my God."

"You took the words right out of my mouth."

They stood there for what felt an eternity, staring at each other and their baby. Shelli's heart began beating out another wild tune. He had come back for her—*for her*! And if the look in John's eyes was any indication, he was happier than she'd ever thought he could be with the knowledge that she was now a package deal.

"Can I hold him?" John asked quietly, his eyes misty.

"Don't cry or I will too!" Shelli promised in a shaky voice. She hoped her smile radiated the warmth and joy she felt. "And of course you can."

He slowly held out his hands. "John," Shelli said, handing him their baby, "meet Johnny."

A single tear rolled down John's cheek as father and son stared at each other, mesmerized. Or at least father did. Son was too busy trying to make a meal out of his dad's tie to get awestruck by anything else. John chuckled, forcing Shelli to grin.

John's gaze flew back to Shelli. "Can I hold you too?"

A sensible woman would have made him grovel for at least another month. Her pride might even have caused her to refuse him altogether, whether still in love with him or not. But Shelli was the world's worst now-former stripper. Sensible wasn't in her vocabulary. Thank God!

"Why, John Calder," Shelli whispered, smiling, "I thought you'd never ask."

Made in the USA
Lexington, KY
15 November 2018